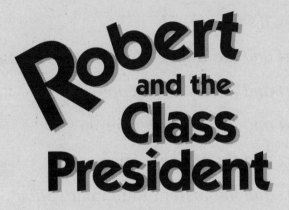

Robert
and the
Class
President

Also by Barbara Seuling

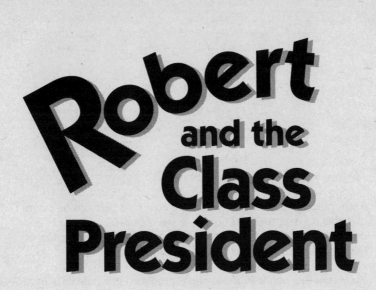

Robert and the Class President

by Barbara Seuling
Illustrated by Paul Brewer

A
LITTLE APPLE
PAPERBACK

SCHOLASTIC INC.

New York Toronto London Auckland Sydney
Mexico City New Delhi Hong Kong Buenos Aires

ISBN 0-439-44379-2

Text copyright © 2003 by Barbara Seuling.
Illustrations copyright © 2003 by Paul Brewer.

All rights reserved. Published by Scholastic Inc., 557 Broadway, New York, NY 10012, by arrangement with Carus Publishing Company. SCHOLASTIC and associated logos are trademarks and/or registered trademarks of Scholastic Inc.

12 11 10 9 8 7   6 7 8/0

Printed in the U.S.A.   40
First Scholastic printing, November 2003

To Meggie Nelson
—B. S.

To Pam Muñoz Ryan and
Helen Foster James
—P. B.

Contents

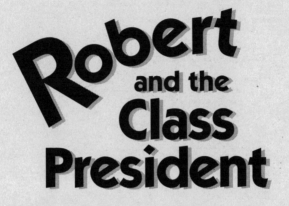

Paul for President!

"**A**nyone home?"

Robert Dorfman had barely opened the door and called out when the big yellow dog galloped up and jumped on him.

"Ooomph!" said Robert, falling to the floor. The dog slurped a wet kiss on his nose.

"Hey, Huckleberry, you're too big to be jumping on me anymore," said Robert, slipping out of his book-bag straps. He pushed his face into the dog's warm fur.

Huckleberry's tail thumped the floor as it wagged back and forth.

On days when no one was home after school, Robert was especially glad he had Huckleberry. He knew his mom had to work at her office sometimes, and that once in a while his dad would stay late at school for a teachers' meeting, and that his brother would always be at practice for some sport or another. It didn't happen very often that all three were out at the same time, but Robert had his own key for those times when it did.

Robert had waited a long time for a dog of his own, and now he had Huckleberry.

Robert got up and, without even taking off his jacket, opened the refrigerator and stared at the container of milk. Was it fresh? He couldn't be sure unless he smelled it.

He didn't feel like smelling it. If it was
bad, the smell would stay in his nose all
afternoon. He decided to have some juice
instead.

Robert gulped down the juice and dropped his jacket on a kitchen chair.

"C'mon, boy," he said. As he thumped up to his room, Huckleberry's toenails tap-tapped on the stairs after him.

Huckleberry bounded onto Robert's bed. Robert plopped down next to him. "Hey, pal!" He stroked Huckleberry's silky coat. Huckleberry rolled over on his back, his legs in the air. Robert laughed.

"I want a picture of you like that," Robert said, getting up to get his camera.

After taking a couple of good shots, Robert gave the dog a belly rub. Right in the middle of rubbing, he had an idea. He jumped up and went to the phone on the landing outside his room. He dialed Paul's number. Paul Felcher was his best friend.

"Paul, I have to take a picture of you," he said.

"Okay. Why?"

"To put on a poster. Kids will see your face and want to vote for you."

Mrs. Bernthal had told them they could hold elections for class president next week. Paul wanted to run for class president, so Robert nominated him and agreed to be his campaign manager. It was his job to help Paul win.

"They will?" said Paul.

"Yes. They will. You've seen the posters for mayor around town, haven't you?"

"Mostly I just see names."

"Your name will be on a poster like that, but a picture of you will make it even better," said Robert. "They have a machine at the mall that can blow up pictures to poster size. We'll make a copy and put it on oak tag. Underneath we'll write in big black letters VOTE FOR PAUL. Then we'll hang it in the hall just outside our classroom. The kids will see it as they walk into the room."

"Okay," said Paul. "How much will it cost? I already spent most of this week's allowance."

"I have some money saved up in my frog bank," said Robert. Grandma Judy had brought all of her bingo winnings to Robert and Charlie on her last visit. "I'll use some of that."

"Thanks. I'll pay you back next week," said Paul.

"That's okay," said Robert.

"I'd better wear my new shirt tomorrow," said Paul.

"Oh. Um . . . I was hoping we could do it today," said Robert.

"I can't today," said Paul. "I have to go to the store with my mom and Nick. Nick needs new shoes, and he won't try them on for anyone but me. And then I have to finish my homework and work on my speech," said Paul. Just before the election, all the candidates had to give speeches about why they should be class president.

One more day wouldn't matter. "Okay," said Robert. He called Huckleberry, and they went downstairs to play ball in the yard.

SUSANNE LEE
CAN DO THE JOB

A New Plan

The next morning, Robert and Paul stared in horror as they walked down the hall to their classroom. Posters with Susanne Lee Rodgers's picture lined the walls. Under each face was the slogan SUSANNE LEE CAN DO THE JOB.

"Oh, no!" said Paul. "She beat us to it!"

"Don't worry," said Robert, trying to sound like a good campaign manager. "We'll think of something else."

Paul just shrugged. "It was dumb to think I could win," he said. "Susanne Lee always wins everything." He looked around at the posters and shrugged. "And she's always—there."

"It wasn't dumb," said Robert as they took their seats at Table Four. "You would make a very good class president."

But Robert knew what Paul meant. Susanne Lee was always in your face. That's what bugged him about her.

She always raised her hand first to answer a question or said what you wanted to say before you had a chance to say it.

She volunteered to be a hall monitor before Mrs. Bernthal even said she needed one.

Her homework was always neat and perfect and tacked up on the bulletin board.

It felt like you never had a chance. When did Susanne Lee Rodgers ever sleep?

They had a week to campaign. Jesse Meiner and Emily Asher were also running for class president. Robert had to tell everyone why they should vote for Paul.

"Let's have a meeting at my house this afternoon," said Robert.

"Okay," said Paul.

Robert didn't know how, but he had to help Paul win this election. His best friend was counting on him.

At Robert's house, Huckleberry met them at the door. The dog danced around, wagging his tail, bringing his chew toy to them.

"What a great welcome!" said Paul.

"Yeah," said Robert. "It's one of the best things about coming home after school. Huckleberry is always happy to see me and ready to play."

In the yard, he and Paul tossed a ball back and forth, challenging Huckleberry to catch it. After Huckleberry ran off with the ball for the third time and he and Paul had to wrestle it away from him, Robert said, "Wait a minute! Don't move!"

He ran into the house and upstairs to his room. He grabbed his camera from his night table. There was still half a roll of film in it. He ran back downstairs and into the yard.

"Stand by the apple tree," he told Paul. Robert snapped a picture. "Now sit on the step." Paul did and smiled into the camera as Robert snapped the next picture.

"I thought it was too late for the poster," said Paul.

"It's still a good idea, so we'll do it," said Robert. "We just have to think of something else, too."

Huckleberry ran by with the ball. Paul grabbed it and tossed it to the dog. Robert needed only one picture of Paul, but he

used up the rest of the film so he could take it in to be developed right away.

At dinner that night, Robert told everyone in his family about the campaign.

"That sounds wonderful," said his mom. "Do you have a slogan?" She scooped up something green from a bowl and plopped it onto Robert's plate.

"Um . . . 'Vote for Paul,'" said Robert.

"That's lame," said Charlie. "You need something catchier."

Robert remembered Susanne Lee's slogan: SUSANNE LEE CAN DO THE JOB.

"I know!" said Charlie. "Vote for Paul Felcher, he's a great belcher."

"Charlie!" said Robert's mom.

"That's not funny, Charlie," Robert's dad said. "Let Robert finish."

Robert told them about the posters and how Susanne Lee Rodgers had had the same idea and had beat them to it.

"You can't blame Susanne Lee for using an idea more efficiently than you did," said Mr. Dorfman. "Having a good idea is not enough. It's how you act on it that counts."

"So what are you planning for your campaign?" asked his mom.

Robert circled his fork around the green stuff and dipped into his mashed potatoes. "We're making a poster," he said, "but I have to get a picture of Paul blown up at the mall. Can you take me over there later?"

His dad cleared his throat. "I'll take you, Tiger," he said.

"Thanks, Dad." Robert put his steak bone over the green stuff, hoping no one would notice.

"Watch out for dirty campaign tricks," said Charlie, who seemed to know something about everything. The trouble was, Charlie often teased Robert, so he never knew what to believe and what not to believe.

"What do you mean?" asked Robert.

"You'll see," said Charlie. "Just keep your eyes open."

"I'm glad you're not discouraged by what happened with Susanne Lee," his dad said, "but you have to do more than make a poster."

"I know," said Robert. Robert just didn't have a clue as to what that might be.

At Quik 1-Hour Foto, they dropped off the film. Then they walked around the mall while they waited. They passed a toy store with the latest action figures in the window, a candy shop with multicolored candies of all kinds, and a gazillion clothing stores. They wandered into and out of a sports equipment store, a drugstore, and a bookstore. Finally, they went back for the pictures.

"These are great, Tiger," said his dad, looking through the envelope. "Did you think of this?" He handed the pictures to Robert.

Robert stared at the photo on top. It was a photo of Paul tossing a ball to Huckleberry.

"Vote for Paul—he's on the ball," said his dad, chuckling.

"Thanks, Dad," said Robert. "That's a great slogan!" It was okay if his dad came up with the slogan. Maybe the photo was an accident, but he did take the picture, after all.

With the help of a store clerk, Robert used the imaging machine to blow up the photo to a humongous size.

As they paid the clerk, Robert had an idea of his own. "Dad, can we stop at the candy place next?"

"Sure, Tiger."

Robert felt like he was on a roll.

Spying

Before they went into their classroom the next day, Robert and Paul stopped in the hall to hang the poster Robert had made the night before. Susanne Lee's posters were gone. What could have persuaded her to take them down?

The picture of Paul tossing a ball to Huckleberry looked good against the orange-colored oak tag he had pasted it on. Underneath it, in huge blue letters, he had printed:

VOTE FOR PAUL— HE'S ON THE BALL!

Later, in the cafeteria, Robert passed around a bag of chocolate-covered malted milk balls. He held out the bag to Melissa Thurm. Melissa reached in and pulled out a candy.

"Vote for Paul—he's on the ball!" he said.

"Thanks," said Melissa. She peeled off the red foil wrapper and popped the candy into her mouth.

Lester didn't wait for them to get to his table. He came bouncing up.

"Have one," said Robert. Lester reached in. "Cool," he said, scraping the foil off and slurping up the chocolate-covered ball.

"Vote for Paul—he's on the ball!" said Robert.

"Those malted milk balls were a great idea," said Paul. "Everyone loves candy."

"Don't think you're so smart, Robert Dorfman!" Robert spun around. Susanne Lee stood there, glaring at him. "You can't give away candy to cover up your sneaky ways."

"What sneaky ways?" Robert asked.

"You know perfectly well what I'm talking about," she said. "You took down all my posters and then put yours up. That was a dirty trick."

Robert was stunned. He never touched Susanne Lee's posters.

"I didn't—" he started to say.

"Just remember, what goes around comes around," she said before she stomped away.

This was terrible. He didn't take down Susanne Lee's posters, but someone did. Who could it be? He remembered Charlie's warning about dirty campaign tricks.

Some of the kids were sucking on malted milk balls when they got back to the classroom. Mrs. Bernthal quieted the sucking noises by tapping a ruler on her desk.

"I'm happy to see you taking the elections so seriously," she said. "You can campaign during recess and at lunch. In the classroom, we have to do our work. So hurry up and finish your candy and break up into your assigned reading groups."

Robert was glad Mrs. Bernthal didn't make everyone throw the malted milk balls into the wastebasket.

It was hard to concentrate on reading, and Robert lost his place twice. When he finally got to read, he made only one mistake. He needed help with the word "machine." He forgot that the *ch* could be pronounced like a *sh*.

At lunchtime, Robert noticed Susanne Lee Rodgers, Kristi Mills, Elizabeth Street, and Melissa Thurm whispering to one another. They kept looking at Robert and Paul. Robert wondered if Susanne Lee was telling them all about the posters. He had to know what they were saying.

"I have to do some spying," he announced, getting up from the lunch table. "Wait here."

Robert took his tray and walked the long way around to the trash barrel, passing the girls' table. Maybe he could hear what

the girls were saying. He thought he heard Kristi say something about a platform, but they stopped talking as he walked by. He could tell by the look on her face that Susanne Lee was still angry.

"Paul, we have to hear what they're saying," said Robert, sliding back onto his bench at their table. "I heard something about a platform. That can't be right."

Paul looked over at the girls. He got up to dump his tray. Robert watched as Paul slowed down and spoke to the girls. Kristi said something to him, but Susanne Lee wouldn't even look at him. Paul finished dumping his tray and came back.

"You're right," he said. "They're building a platform."

"Why?" asked Robert. He looked over at the girls. They were leaning over their table and whispering again.

Paul shrugged. "I don't know. They said it's something all the candidates do."

Robert lowered his voice. "Why do you think the girls are building a platform? They could be trying to trick us. They're mad at us for something we didn't do. Charlie said we should be careful."

Paul looked puzzled. "I don't know. Maybe Charlie is right. I never heard about making a platform before. Maybe it's to stand on when you give your speech."

All afternoon they tried to find out more, but the girls weren't talking. It must be pretty important if they were keeping it such a big secret.

Just to be sure, Robert asked Jesse if he had a platform.

"Sure. All the candidates have one. Don't you have yours?"

"Yeah, I do," said Robert. He suddenly

felt itchy, just like when he was doing a hard math problem.

"We'd better get working on ours, then," Robert told Paul when they were alone. "Or else I just told a big lie."

The Platform

At Paul's house that afternoon, they searched for lumber. They went down to the basement. Paul's dad sometimes built or repaired things there. They found a couple of boards and scraps of wood, a hammer and nails, and a hot-glue gun.

"This is like playing with blocks again," said Robert.

"Yeah. Except this time we really don't want them to fall down," said Paul.

"How high is a platform?" asked Robert.

"I guess high enough so everyone can see you when you're giving your speech," answered Paul.

They found two long pieces of lumber that looked good for making the base of the platform. They laid the pieces down and put two boards across them. The boards were not the same length. Later, they could saw them even. They hammered the boards to the base.

"It needs to be higher," said Robert. Sure enough, the platform almost disappeared into the grass.

"Okay." Paul picked up some pieces of wood and the hot-glue gun. Gluing one piece to another, he made four stacks of scraps. He glued the stacks to the four corners of the platform, like legs.

They stood back and looked at the platform. It was crooked. One side was higher than the other. Paul used the hot-glue gun

to stick extra pieces of wood to the lower side. That evened out the platform, but when Paul stood on it, it wobbled.

"Whooooa-oo-oa!" he cried, balancing himself. "You have to stand with your feet wide apart so it doesn't wobble."

"Okay," said Robert. "You can do that."

Paul stared at the platform. "We should even these boards out," he said. He went down to the basement and came back with a saw. He tried to cut the end off the longer board, but the saw blade kept sticking in the wood.

"My dad will kill me if I break his saw," he said, trying to jiggle the saw loose.

"Maybe we'd better leave it alone," said Robert.

"What are we supposed to do with it now?" asked Paul, finally getting the saw out of the wood.

The construction looked more like a raft with feet than a platform.

"I don't know," said Robert. "We'll have to watch what the others do with theirs. Let's keep it in your backyard for now."

"Okay," said Paul.

They cleaned up the mess they had made in the yard and basement. Afterward, using Paul's art supplies, they cut 20 campaign buttons out of thick paper.

As Robert cut, Paul printed on each of them: VOTE FOR PAUL—HE'S ON THE BALL with a black marker.

By the time Robert went home, his thumb was sore from cutting out all those buttons.

Slogans and
Handouts

Before Mrs. Bernthal asked the class to settle down so she could take attendance, Robert and Paul handed out the paper buttons with Paul's slogan printed on them. They also gave each person a safety pin to pin on the button.

Susanne Lee had already handed out long pink strips that had her name written on them with a purple glitter pen.

"Have a bookmark," she said as she handed each kid a strip. "And remember to vote for me. I can do the job." She thrust one at Robert.

Joey Rizzo and Matt Blakey were helping Jesse tape a banner to the wall outside the classroom under the bulletin board. It said, WIN WITH JESSE.

Emily Asher didn't carry a sign or go around or hand out anything. Everyone knew Emily would make a good class president.

Melissa Thurm smiled at Paul. "So what about your platform?" she asked. "I haven't heard anything about it." Kristi Mills looked on.

"We have one," said Robert, coming to Paul's rescue. "It's great. It's in Paul's backyard."

"Very funny," said Kristi Mills. "But keeping it a secret is dumb. How will anyone know why they should vote for you? Isn't it time you shared it?"

Robert wasn't sure—was this a trick? How could they share a platform? They would never all fit. Besides, no one else showed him their platform. They didn't even say where they kept theirs.

At recess, Susanne Lee walked over to Robert and Paul, her hair bouncing.

"So, are you still not telling about your platform?" she said. "It must be pretty bad if you're keeping it a secret." Kristi and Melissa giggled.

"No," said Robert. "It's not a secret. It's a little wobbly, but it's good." He turned to Paul. "Right, Paul?"

"Right," said Paul.

"So what is it?" asked Susanne Lee. She put her hand on her hip.

"You first," said Robert, putting his hand on his hip, too.

"Okay," said Susanne Lee. She stood as straight as a soldier. "I will start an honor roll for kids with the highest grades."

Robert had a sinking feeling in his stomach.

"I will listen to the problems of anyone in the class and see if I can help solve them," said Susanne Lee.

Robert knew that he must have misunderstood what "platform" meant.

Susanne Lee went on. "As class president, I will help keep the class quiet when Mrs. Bernthal has to leave the room."

Robert and Paul exchanged looks. Paul must have figured it out now, too. He rolled his eyes, making Robert laugh.

Now Susanne Lee put both hands on her hips. "What's so funny?"

"Nothing," said Paul. "I was just thinking . . . about something funny my little brother said." Robert had to struggle not to crack up, thinking of Nick's latest words: "pickle face."

Susanne Lee sighed.

Robert put his hands in his pockets, trying to look cool. "That was very good," he said.

"Well?" demanded Susanne Lee. "What about yours?"

"Oh," said Robert. "We'll have it ready tomorrow."

It wasn't a lie. They would have it ready tomorrow. They just hadn't written it down yet.

Susanne Lee sucked her teeth and walked away. "Pitiful," she muttered.

Robert swallowed hard. That was a close one!

In Your Face

The three o'clock bell rang. Robert and Paul ran two blocks to Paul's house. It was two blocks closer to school than Robert's.

"Hi, boys," said Mrs. Felcher as they flew by her and into the living room.

"Hi!" they shouted back.

"What's the big rush?" Mrs. Felcher asked, following them.

"We have to look something up," said Paul, pulling the dictionary from the bookshelf. He flipped through the pages and stopped. "Platform," he said. He read out loud, "A platform is 'a stage or floor for performers or speakers.'"

"Well, that's what we have," said Robert.

"Wait. There's another meaning," said Paul. "It also says it's 'a statement of principles of a political party.'"

"Oh, no!" said Robert. "That's the one they're talking about!"

"It's a good thing we didn't tell them about our platform," said Paul.

"Yeah," said Robert. "They would never stop laughing if they found out."

Paul put the book back on the shelf, and they ran out to the yard.

Robert stared at the platform. He stood on it and rocked. "Whoooaa!" he said. "I'm glad you never had to use it. It could make you seasick."

They dragged the platform out into the center of the yard. Paul used the back end of the hammer to try to pry the boards loose.

"I saw my dad do this," he explained. They tugged and pried until their arms hurt. This was even harder than putting the platform together. That platform just didn't want to come apart.

"We just have to get it small enough to put out with the trash," said Paul. "My dad is already going to kill me for wasting his lumber. He'd kill me more if I left a mess."

"You always say your dad will kill you," said Robert. "I bet he wouldn't really kill you."

Paul thought about that. "Well, maybe he wouldn't exactly kill me," he said. "But he'd be mad."

"I never saw your dad mad," said Robert. His own father was pretty calm, except when things got out of order. He was a neat freak. Maybe a book would be put back in the wrong place in the book-case. If he found it, then he'd lecture them on the importance of putting things back where they found them.

"Yeah, my dad doesn't get mad much. I just know he wouldn't like it, though, and that's enough for me." Paul was just like his father. He never got into fights or got really mad at anyone.

At last, they were finished. They went inside to wash up.

"We have to write out our platform," said Paul, soaping his hands in the running water at the bathroom sink.

"Yeah," said Robert, following right behind Paul.

Mrs. Felcher had milk and cookies ready for them when they were cleaned up. They sat down at the kitchen table.

Robert pried open a cookie and licked the cream filling from the inside. Paul got up and tore a piece of paper off the message pad by the telephone. He took a pencil from the drawer. He put them on the table.

"Let's start," said Paul.

"What would you do as class president?" asked Robert, picking up the pencil.

Paul shrugged. "I don't know," he said. "I've never been a class president before."

"You can make sure everyone does their job, like taking care of the animals." Robert hated it when someone forgot to clean the cages or give the animals food and clean water every day.

"That's good," said Paul. "Our classroom would smell better, too."

Robert wrote it down.

   1. MAKE SURE EVERYONE DOES THEIR
     JOB

"You can ask for more class trips," said Robert.

"And more special projects and art supplies," said Paul. He loved to make things
and paint.

Robert wrote down:

    2. MORE CLASS TRIPS

    3. MORE SPECIAL PROJECKS

"What about being friendly to new kids?" asked Robert.

"There are no new kids," said Paul.

"But what if we got one?" asked Robert. "We could help them learn about our class and where things are."

"That's good," said Paul. "Write that down."

Robert wrote:

4. BE HELPFUL TO NEW KIDS

"Susanne Lee said she would do things that would make our class better," said Paul. "We have to think of more things like that."

"These things will make our class better," Robert said.

"It has to be something really important," said Paul.

"Yeah," said Robert, tapping his pencil. "Like making Mrs. Bernthal proud."

"Like keeping Susanne Lee out of our faces," added Paul.

Robert laughed. "We can put her in a suit of armor."

Paul laughed, too. "Or build a portable fence around her that she has to take everywhere with her."

They cracked themselves up. Finally, they stopped laughing.

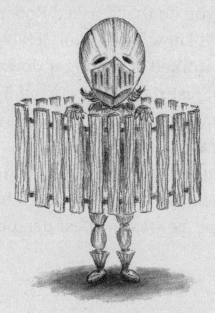

"But she *is* really smart," said Robert.

"I know," said Paul. "But sometimes other kids want to say something. Even if they're not always right, they should get a chance."

There was a pause.

"I know," said Paul. "I will make a rule that no one can raise their hand all the time."

"Can you do that?" asked Robert.

"I don't know," said Paul. "I'll try."

They worked at writing it down until it came out just right. Robert read it back.

5. MAKE SURE EVERYONE GETS A CHANSE

It sounded good. Now, Paul had to write his speech. He had to convince his classmates that he was the best person for the job.

Three Different Beginnings

It was Saturday, and Paul was still working on his speech.

Robert could hardly sit still. He called Paul.

"Hi," he said. "How is the speech going?"

"It's hard. Whenever I say something about what I will do as class president, it sounds like I'm bragging."

"Yeah. Susanne Lee has no trouble doing that."

"Exactly. Maybe she should be class president because she doesn't mind being pushy." Paul sounded discouraged.

"Why don't you come over and we'll work on it together?" said Robert. "We can also take some time out to play with Huckleberry. He needs some exercise."

"Okay," said Paul. "I'll bring what I have so far."

"Good."

Paul arrived with a large envelope. He took out several pages and made three piles. "This is my speech," he said.

"What are the three piles?" asked Robert.

"Well, it's one speech, but there are three different ways to begin it."

"Wow." Robert had no idea how difficult it was to write a speech. "Why don't you read all of them. Then we can choose the best one."

There was a knock on the door. "Hi,

boys," said Mrs. Dorfman. "Would you like to have dinner with us tonight, Paul?"

Robert looked at Paul. That would be great! Dinner wouldn't be as good as dinner at the Felchers, but it would be fun, anyway.

"We're going to have take-out Chinese food tonight," added his mom, as if reading his mind.

"Yes!" said Robert. It was getting even better. His mom wasn't cooking.

"Sure," said Paul. "Thanks. I'll have to call my mom."

Paul made his phone call, and Mrs. Felcher said it would be fine. Then Mrs. Dorfman took the phone from Paul.

"My husband will drive Paul home," she promised.

Robert winked at Paul. "Limousine service," he whispered. Paul nodded and smiled.

They went back to working on Paul's

speech. Huckleberry lay across the bed on his back, all four paws in the air, fast asleep.

"He's smiling," said Paul.

"Yeah. He smiles," said Robert. "Pepperoni smiled, too. People say dogs don't smile, but I know two dogs who do."

Paul read the first speech out loud. "As your class president, I want to make sure everyone in our class is treated fair and square."

Robert applauded as Paul finished. "That's good," he said.

Paul read the second version.

"You know how it is when you have something to say and you don't get a chance to say it?" he began.

Robert couldn't believe it. The first one was good, but this beginning was even better.

"Okay, here goes," said Paul, reading from the third set of papers.

"What you have to say matters." He went on. Robert was mesmerized.

This one was even better than the first two. Wait a minute. He needed to hear the first one again. And maybe the second.

"They all sound good," said Robert.

"See what I mean?" said Paul.

It was hard deciding which one to use. "Bring them downstairs when we have dinner. My family can help us decide."

"Okay," said Paul, clipping together the three sets of pages and slipping them back into the envelope.

Huckleberry Votes

Huckleberry woke up and started prancing around the room.

"Huckleberry wants to go out," said Robert. "Come on. We'll play catch with him."

They thumped down the stairs, one after the other, Huckleberry click-clicking in the lead.

It was good to be out in the crisp November air. There were still a few leaves on the apple tree, but most of them were in a pile on the side of the yard. Huckleberry loved running into the leaves after

the ball. Before long, all three of them were
diving into the leaves.

Mrs. Dorfman called them in for dinner.
They were glad to come in and get warm.
Robert led Paul to the bathroom, where
they washed up.

When they sat down at the table, Robert was glad not to see the usual fish sticks or chicken nuggets.

There were several large bowls set out. One contained shrimp and vegetables, another had sliced-up beef and broccoli, another had chunks of chicken with sesame seeds on them, and another had steaming rice.

In smaller bowls were crispy noodles and fortune cookies. All the smells made Robert's nose twitch happily.

"Dig in," said Mr. Dorfman.

The food tasted as good as it looked.

"We never have Chinese food at our house," said Paul. "This is great."

Robert had eaten at Paul's house lots of times. Paul's mom made great food. It was nice to know his own mom could have great food, too, even if she didn't cook it herself.

As the dishes were cleared from the table, Robert asked Paul to take out his speech. Everyone hung around to hear it, except for Charlie.

"My friends will be here to pick me up in ten minutes," he said. "I have to go." It was Saturday night. Nobody expected Charlie to stay home.

"Be home by eleven," Mrs. Dorfman reminded him.

Charlie grunted, "Okay," and left.

Mr. and Mrs. Dorfman pulled their chairs back from the table and sat, listening. "The floor is yours," said Mr. Dorfman.

"This is Number One," Paul began. "It's the first one I wrote." Nervously, he looked around. He cleared his throat and began.

"As your class president. I want to make sure everyone in our class is treated fair and square. . . ."

When Paul finished his whole speech, everyone applauded, and Huckleberry wagged his tail.

"Just one thing," said Mr. Dorfman, still clapping. "It's a very good speech, but you should say 'fairly and squarely,' not 'fair and square.'"

"Oh. Fairly and squarely," repeated Paul. "Thanks."

Paul picked up another set of papers. "Number Two," he announced. "This one is like I'm talking to a friend. I thought it might sound better that way." He began.

"You know how it is when you have something to say and you don't get a chance to say it? . . ."

There was another round of applause and a tail wag when he finished.

"Then," said Paul, "after I wrote the others, I thought maybe it should sound more important and be stronger. So I wrote this." Paul read version Number Three.

"What you have to say matters! . . ."

There was more clapping as Paul put his paper down and took a small bow.

Huckleberry stood up, wagging his tail.

"Okay," said Robert. "We have to vote on which speech Paul should give tomorrow. Raise your hand for Number One."

Mr. Dorfman raised his hand. "That was an excellent speech, Paul," he said. "You told your classmates what you planned to do and why you felt it was important."

Robert wrote under Speech #1: 1

"How many votes for the second one?" he asked. His mom raised her hand.

"I liked the friendly way you got the kids to think about what it's like to be left out," she said.

Robert wrote under Speech #2 : 1

"Number Three?" he asked. Robert raised his own hand.

He wrote under Speech #3: 1

"Paul, how do you vote?"

"I don't know. That's my problem. I can't decide." Paul looked worried.

Huckleberry wagged his tail furiously.

"We have a tie," said Robert. He looked at Huckleberry. "Come here, boy."

Huckleberry went up to Robert and sat, his tail sweeping the floor from left to right.

"Okay, stay here," Robert commanded. He handed the papers for Speech Number One to his dad, those for Speech Number Two to his mom, and the last set, for Speech Number Three, to Paul.

"Now, when I say 'go,' each of you call Huckleberry. The one he goes to has the speech he votes for."

All three lined up with their speeches in hand. At the signal, there was a commotion of sounds and motions.

"Come here, Huck." Mrs. Dorfman bent over and made baby sounds.

"Here boy, this way, come on." Mr. Dorfman used his deepest voice.

"Aw, Huckleberry, c'mon over here." Paul waved the speech as though it were a toy.

"Huck, Huck, attaboy, come here."

"Hey, old fella, come to me."

"Huckleberry, come!"

"C'mon, boy!"

"Huckleberry! Here!"

"Here, sweetie, come to Mama."

The confused dog did not know which way to turn, but at last he walked over and sat at Paul's feet.

Robert shouted. "Huckleberry voted!" he cried. "It's Speech Number Three!"

IF I AM
ELECTED
CLASS
PRESIDENT
I PROMISE TO...

Promises

Jesse, Joey, and Matt did not look happy on Monday morning. They stared at Robert and Paul as they walked into the classroom.

"What's going on?" Robert asked Vanessa, who sat at Table Four with them.

"Their banner is gone," said Vanessa. "They think you took it."

"What? Why do they think that?" said Robert.

"Because you took down Susanne Lee's posters," said Vanessa.

60

"We did not!" shouted Robert. "We didn't take down any posters or banner!"

The other kids just stared back at them. What could they do? Everyone believed they did it. That certainly wouldn't win Paul any votes.

Mrs. Bernthal took the attendance. "Excellent!" she said when she knew everyone was there.

"Today, class," she said, "we will hear some speeches. Will the candidates for class president please come up front?"

Emily, Jesse, Susanne Lee, and Paul went up and stood in front of Mrs. Bernthal's desk.

Mrs. Bernthal complimented them on their campaigns. "You ran good campaigns," she said. Robert thought he saw Susanne Lee whisper, "Cheaters!" to Kristi, but he couldn't be sure.

"And no matter who gets the most votes, you are all winners to me," she said.

Jesse and Susanne Lee stared at Robert and Paul.

It wasn't fair. Robert and Paul were being blamed for something they didn't do.

"May the best person win," Mrs. Bernthal said.

Emily went first.

"If I am elected class president," she began, "I promise to see that the girls are included in all the sports that the boys are—softball, basketball, running, etcetera." She paused. Then she added, "And I promise that boys will have to jump rope and be cheerleaders."

The boys gasped. The girls clapped. Someone even whistled.

Emily continued her speech and concluded with, "And so a vote for Emily is a vote for equal rights."

All the girls applauded vigorously. The boys just sat and stared.

"Thank you, Emily," said Mrs. Bernthal. "Jesse, you're next."

Jesse was wearing a suit and tie. He never missed a chance to show that he was cool. He promised that he would ask Mrs. Bernthal for more science projects. He promised he would work for a class trip to the Liberty Science Museum. He promised that he would do something about stolen lunches and fighting on the playground.

After Jesse, Susanne Lee came forward. Her hair bounced with every step she took. She wore big pink hair bows.

Susanne Lee promised the class they would have 100 percent attendance every day. Robert imagined her pulling sick kids out of bed to drag them to school.

Susanne Lee promised to help kids who had problems with their math and spelling and reading. Robert gritted his teeth as she talked. He remembered sitting in a reading group with bossy Susanne Lee as the leader.

"As class president," Susanne Lee said, "I promise to see that our class behaves when Mrs. Bernthal leaves the room."

The boys groaned.

Paul was up last, wearing his favorite shirt and his "rocket pocket" jeans. He had

painted rocket ships on the back pockets of his jeans.

Robert had listened to Paul's speech a gazillion times, so he knew it by heart. He almost held his breath until it was over. Paul did not make any mistakes.

Paul finished with Robert's favorite line, "It's not what we say today that matters, but what we do tomorrow." That was the line they worked on the most together. They had added "today" and "tomorrow" at the very last minute.

All the speeches were good. It was impossible to guess who would win. The boys probably wouldn't vote for Emily, but a lot of girls would. Would the class believe all the promises that were made? Would anyone vote for Paul? It was going to be torture for Robert waiting for tomorrow to come.

Election Day

Mrs. Bernthal showed them how to use their ballot to vote.

"There is a list of the candidates' names." She held up a piece of paper. "In front of each name is a little box. Put a check mark next to the name of the person you are voting for. Then fold the paper in half like this," she said as she showed them, "and put it in the box on my desk." Mrs. Bernthal pointed to a cardboard carton with BALLOTS printed in black marker on the side.

"Can we vote twice?" shouted Lester Willis. Lester always called out without raising his hand first.

"You will get only one ballot," Mrs. Bernthal answered. "And you may check off only one name. If there are multiple check marks, the ballot will be voided." Robert liked the way Mrs. Bernthal talked to them as though they were grown-ups.

"I will count the ballots," said Mrs. Bernthal, "and I will announce the winner."

Mrs. Bernthal commended them again for an excellent campaign. Robert wondered if she knew the kids thought he and Paul had pulled down the posters and banner.

After everyone had deposited their ballots in the box, Mrs. Bernthal picked up the box and shook it. She took the lid off and began counting votes at her desk.

After slowly and carefully taking out each paper, Mrs. Bernthal read it and put it

in a pile. Robert watched as she put one
paper in one pile, two in the next, one in
the next, and so on.

There were four piles. When the box
was empty, she counted each pile.

"Your class president is . . . Susanne Lee," said Mrs. Bernthal.

Robert let his breath out. He looked at Paul. Paul didn't look upset.

"This is how the voting went," said Mrs. Bernthal, going up to the chalkboard. She picked up a piece of chalk and wrote:

Susanne Lee 7
Paul Felcher 6
Jesse Meiner 4
Emily Asher 3

Robert's eyebrows went up. He looked over at Paul. Paul's mouth was open. It looked like he was saying, "Wow," but without any sound coming out.

Once the results of the election were announced, Mrs. Bernthal asked them to work on their special projects. They were studying Native Americans. Robert was constructing a pueblo out of papier mâché. Paul was in the back of the room, painting a miniature tepee.

Robert walked over to see the tepee. Paul had painted a running deer on it.

Vanessa, sitting nearby, was making a pot with coils of clay.

"Congratulations," she said to Paul. "You almost won."

"Thanks," said Paul.

"That's true," said Robert, turning to Paul. "Susanne Lee had only one vote more than you."

"Yeah. That must mean the kids didn't really think we took down Susanne Lee's posters and Jesse's banner." Paul grinned. "We had a good campaign," he said. "It must have been our platform."

That cracked Robert up. Paul laughed so hard his paintbrush spattered one of the horses he was painting. Vanessa just stared at him.

"It's a spotted pony," Paul told her.

That did it. Robert laughed so hard he had to go to the bathroom. He got the hall pass from Mrs. Bernthal and ran out the door.

Lester Willis was in the boys' bathroom when Robert got there. He was still wearing his VOTE FOR PAUL—HE'S ON THE BALL button.

"Yo! Robert!" he greeted him.

Robert never knew what to expect from Lester. He had been bullied by Lester once, but that had changed. They were not exactly friends, but Lester didn't bother him anymore.

"Hi, Lester," he said, doing what he came to do.

"How'd you like those elections?" Lester asked.

"They turned out great," Robert answered. He added, "We almost won."

"Yeah," said Lester with a big grin on his face. "I wanted you to win."

"Thanks." Robert went over to the sink to wash his hands.

"I should have done more stuff to help," said Lester.

"What do you mean?" asked Robert.

"You know . . . the posters and things," said Lester.

"What about the posters and things?"

Lester grinned again. "Wasn't it funny how they kept disappearing, all except yours?"

Robert dried his hands in a hurry. He was afraid of what Lester was about to say. "You mean . . . you . . . ?" He couldn't finish his sentence.

"I had to," said Lester. "I wanted you guys to win."

Robert couldn't speak. What could he say? He certainly couldn't say thank you for doing something like that.

"I . . . I . . . have to get back," he said. He forced a smile.

"Okay. See you later," said Lester.

Robert raced back to the classroom and told Paul.

"It's a good thing we didn't win," said Paul. "That would be like stealing."

"Yeah," said Robert. "It probably wouldn't even count. We'd have to do it over."

"Really?" said Paul.

"Charlie says there are lots of dirty tricks during elections." Robert watched Paul paint a zigzag design around the top of the tepee. "But that's not the way I'd want to win."

"Yeah, me neither." Paul painted his last zig.

There was a long quiet moment.

"We'd better talk to Lester," said Robert.

"Yeah," said Paul, putting down his paintbrush. "We can't let him think he did a good thing."

Dirty Tricks

"Hey, Lester, can we talk to you?" said Robert, walking up to Lester's table. Paul was right beside him.

Lester looked up from the clay pot he was making. "Yo, guys. What's up?"

"It's about the elections," said Paul.

"Cool, huh? You almost won."

"Um, Lester," said Robert, "that's what we want to talk to you about. We know you wanted us to win . . . but . . . well . . . we didn't want to win that way."

76

Lester looked blank. "Huh? What do you mean? What way?"

"By playing dirty tricks on the other candidates," said Paul. "We only want to win because the kids think we can do the best job."

Butterflies flew around in Robert's stomach. He couldn't help remembering a fight he once had with Lester. Lester had almost smothered him by sitting on him.

Lester's forehead wrinkled. "I just wanted to help," he said.

"Yeah, I know," said Robert. "And we're glad you were on our side. But we aren't glad that now some of the kids think we're . . ."

". . . sneaky," said Paul. "If people think we took down their posters, they would never trust us on anything ever again."

Lester didn't get mad. He just looked puzzled. Robert felt sorry for him.

Suddenly, Lester pushed his chair back and got up. He walked over to Table 3.

"Yo, Susanne Lee!" he said. "I took down your posters."

"Oh, really?" Susanne Lee shouted back at Lester. She stood up to face him. "So they asked you to do their dirty work, did they? You're pitiful, Lester Willis! You're all pitiful!"

"No!" said Lester, even louder. "They didn't ask me. I just did it. I didn't want you to win."

Susanne Lee looked surprised and sat back down.

By now, Mrs. Bernthal was interested. "May I ask what's going on?" she asked.

"Nothing," said Lester. "I just had something to tell Susanne Lee."

"Well, good," said Mrs. Bernthal. "Perhaps we can say what we have to a little more quietly."

Lester went back to Table 5 and sat
down. "Thanks," said Robert, letting out
his breath finally. Lester nodded as he

slapped a piece of clay in his hands and continued to work on his pot.

Wow. Robert never knew Lester was so brave. It wasn't just confessing. He had stood up to Susanne Lee!

Everybody
Listened

Huckleberry met Robert and Paul at the door. Nobody else was home. Robert's mom worked at the travel agency on Tuesdays. Robert wished someone was home so he could tell them all about the elections.

"Hey, Huckleberry," said Robert, dropping his book bag. "We almost won!" He scratched the dog behind his ears.

Huckleberry broke away from Robert, went racing into the other room, and came back with a cloth doll that he dropped at Paul's feet.

"Your victory present," said Robert. "He takes out his stinkiest toys for special occasions."

Paul dropped his book bag on the floor and reached for the doll. "Yuck!" said Paul, touching it. "It's gross!"

"I told you," said Robert.

Paul made a face as he tried to play tug-of-war with the disgusting doll.

"Hey, Huck, let's go outside," he said. The dog dropped the toy and ran for the door. "It worked!" said Paul,

In the yard, Robert picked up Huckleberry's ball and tossed it to Paul.

"I came close to being class president," said Paul to Huckleberry. "And you helped. You chose my speech." Huckleberry grabbed the ball and ran around the yard with it.

"You know," said Paul, watching Huckleberry run, "I still can't believe so many kids voted for me."

Robert sat on the swing and pushed a little. "I can't believe Lester Willis told everyone what he did."

"Yeah," said Paul. "I think he finally got it—that winning fair is the only way to win."

"You know the best thing?" said Paul. "Everybody listened to what we had to say. Even Susanne Lee. So maybe she'll think about giving everybody else a chance."

"Yeah. That's right," said Robert. "Maybe now Susanne Lee will not win every single contest and get every word right on her spelling tests, too."

"And next time, when Mrs. Bernthal asks a question, she won't be the first one to throw up her hand to answer."

There was a pause. Huckleberry came over and sat down, staring at Paul, then at Robert. Paul looked at Robert. Robert looked at Paul.

"It'll NEVER HAPPEN!" they said at the same time.

Collapsing in the grass, they laughed so hard they could hardly get up. They loved cracking themselves up.